SHOE SHAKES

Written by Loris Lesynski

Illustrated by Michael Martchenko

annick press
toronto • new york • vancouver

Reading **Shoe Shakes**
out loud? Remember to put
a lot of **bounce** in your voice
and have as much fun as
you can with the **beat.**

Loris

What's Inside

The Wake-Up Shake-Up

It's morning!
   And morning
      as everyone knows
   begins with a wiggle
      in everyone's toes.

   Your knees need to jiggle,
      your arms need to spin.

A wonderful way for a day
   to begin!

Your shoulders need bouncing.
   Your back needs a pat.
You s-t-r-e-t-c-h and you s-t-r-e-t-c-h
   till you're perfectly flat.

4

Reading out loud? Put your child's name in the last line, for instance "Michael's up and awake" or ""Sarah's up and awake."

It's morning!
It's morning!
Rock, wriggle and shake.
Let *everyone* know that
you're up and awake.

The waking-up shake
makes a **whoosh!**
as it goes
up, down, around you
from bottom to nose.

Shoe Shakes

Run run runningshoes

fly fly flyingshoes

which shoes

will I choose

will I choose today?

Jump jump jumpingshoes

tip toe tapping shoes

which shoes

should I choose

should I choose today?

You decide
   to skip or slide.
Slow or quick?
   You take your pick.
Lots of ways
   to move your feet
up the stairs
   and down the street
round the corners
   round the block
twenty million ways
   to walk.

Hop or march or sway or stride,

   fast or slowly, you decide.

Here's the news: it's always you

   who chooses what your shoes'll do.

BUT WHAT IF...

7

...my shoes shook me?

8

And your shoes shook you?

And they pulled you to the park!

And they zoomed you to the zoo!

11

And they swung you up
the stairs...

...bouncing like a kangaroo?

AND THEN...

…if my shoes
shook *me*…
and your shoes
shook *you*…

14

…what would the **shoes** of the lions and the tigers and the bears and the birds and the penguins and the piglets and the monkeys do?

NOTH

Because lions and tigers and bears and birds an don't **WEAR** shoes!

16

Was this a silly story? **Yes!**

Was any of it true? **Well...**

Can *anybody's* shoes shake them

or even me or you?

Noooooo...

Who **shakes** and **leaps** and **jumps** all day?

It's **you**, that's who, you run and play.

A shoe can't shake by itself, **no way!**

A shoe can't shake

no, a shoe can't shake

a shoe can't shake

by itself.

And now, some *more* poems...

18

Toot Toot!

some dogs woof

some dogs bark

mine goes **toot! toot! toot!**

in the park

some birds chirp

some birds tweet

mine goes **toot! toot!**

loud and sweet

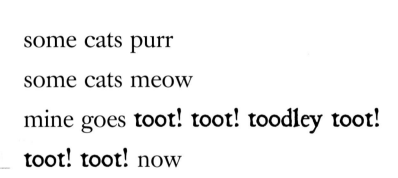

some cats purr

some cats meow

mine goes **toot! toot! toodley toot!**

toot! toot! now

The Boot Boot Bounce

Rain boots

snow boots

go boots

go!

20

Slide boots

glide boots

fast boots

slow.

On boots

off boots

boots in a row.

See you again

tomorrow!

21

Feet Thoughts

Cats have fur feet.

Dogs have four.

An octopus has

even more.

Snakes are footless.

So are fish.

They don't step, just

swish swish swish.

Snowshoes

Snowshoes sound like
  shoes made of snow.
Could that be so?
  I think not, no.

    Snowshoes go
      on top of snow,
      on mountains high,
        in valleys low.

  Through snowy forests,
    on trails of ice.

  On frozen fields.
    The Arctic twice.

  Don't have snowshoes?
      What do you think
        would happen then...?

23

You'd sink!

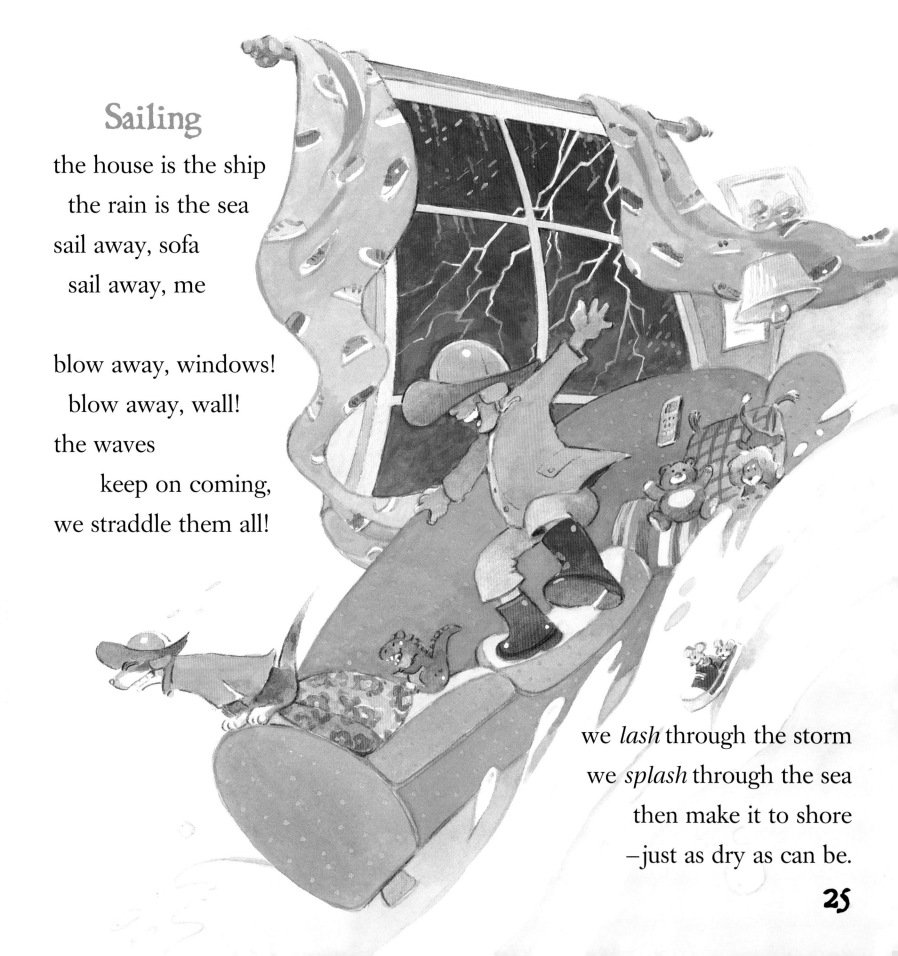

Sailing

the house is the ship
the rain is the sea
sail away, sofa
sail away, me

blow away, windows!
blow away, wall!
the waves
keep on coming,
we straddle them all!

we *lash* through the storm
we *splash* through the sea
then make it to shore
—just as dry as can be.

25

Shoe Search

Red shoes
yellow shoes
green shoes
blue

big shoes
little shoes
three shoes
two

daddy shoes
baby shoes
girl's shoes
boy's

clown shoes
brown shoes
curly shoes
toy's

26

what about...
banana shoes?

what about... *ballet*?

if we started counting shoes
we'd count till Saturday!

muddy shoes

shiny shoes

purple shoes with spots

even seven shoes that someone used
for flowerpots

Ant's-Eye View

The ant on my ankle
    looks up at my knee.
I think that he's thinking,
    "That's too far for me."
But he starts up my leg
    with his little ant feet,
going fast as he can
    like my leg
is a street.

It tickles a little.
    He makes it, and then,
he runs down my legstreet
again.

Rainy Day Dance

busy rainy drizzle day
all the sun has gone away
stay inside and puzzle play
but when's it going to stop
stop
when's it going to stop?

when the rain is gone again
boots and jacket on again
sun is shining strong again
now we run and jump and leap
and skip and slide and hop
hop
skip and slide
and hop.

29

If You Had a Magic Shoe...

What would you do
   if you had a magic shoe?
An amazing magic shoe!
   Would you make a wish or two?

   Would you wish it were a car,
      bright and shiny as a star?
         Would you drive it fast and far?

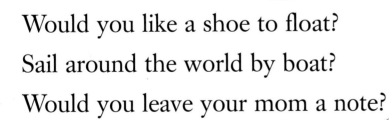

Would you like a shoe to float?
Sail around the world by boat?
Would you leave your mom a note?

Would your magic shoeplane fly
gliding freely in the sky
seeing mountains from up high?

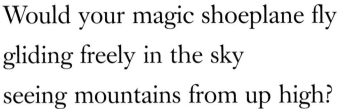

How about a shoe that hopped
by itself and never stopped?

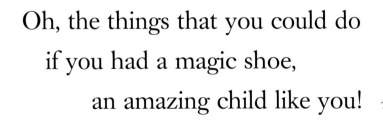

Oh, the things that you could do
if you had a magic shoe,
an amazing child like you!

Let imagination soar.
Can you think of any more?

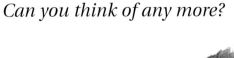

Remembering when they were little, we dedicate this book...

to Erik and Mara to Alex and Lucas
–with lots of love, Loris –from Grampa Michael

© 2007 Loris Lesynski (text)
© 2007 Michael Martchenko (illustrations)

Design/Loris Lesynski, *Laugh Lines Design*

Annick Press Ltd.

We acknowledge the support of the Canada Council for the Arts, the Ontario Arts Council, and the Government of Canada through the Book Publishing Industry Development Program (BPIDP) for our publishing activities.

Cataloging in Publication

Lesynski, Loris
   Shoe shakes / written by Loris Lesynski; art by Michael Martchenko.

Poems.
ISBN 978-1-55451-106-8 (bound)
ISBN 978-1-55451-105-1 (pbk.)

   1. Children's poetry, Canadian (English). I. Martchenko, Michael
II. Title.
PS8573.E79S56 2007   jC811'.54   C2007-902349-5

The art in this book was rendered in pencil, watercolor and gouache.
The poems were typeset in Caslon and the titles in Blackbeard.

Distributed in Canada by:
   Firefly Books
   66 Leek Crescent,
   Richmond Hill, ON
   L4B 1H1

   Printed and bound in China

Published in the U.S.A. by:
Annick Press (U.S.) Ltd.
Distributed in the U.S.A. by:
   Firefly Books (U.S.) Inc.
   P.O. Box 1338, Ellicott Station,
   Buffalo, NY 14205

Loris loves getting letters.
Send your messages, questions or comments directly to the author any time:
Loris Lesynski, c/o Annick Press, 15 Patricia Avenue, Toronto, Ontario Canada M2M 1H9.
Or you can e-mail her at loris@lorislesynski.com

Visit Loris's website at **www.lorislesynski.com**